LASSO LOU AND COWBOY McCOY

Barbara Larmon Failing

pictures by Tedd Arnold

Dial Books for Young Readers New York

Published by Dial Books for Young Readers
A division of Penguin Young Readers Group
345 Hudson Street
New York, New York 10014

Ingram 10-21-03 $16.99/9.65

Text copyright © 2003 by Barbara Larmon Failing
Pictures copyright © 2003 by Tedd Arnold

Typography by Nancy R. Leo-Kelly
Text set in Cloister
Manufactured in China on acid-free paper
1 3 5 7 9 10 8 6 4 2

34322 000 215036

Library of Congress Cataloging-in-Publication Data
Failing, Barbara Larmon.
Lasso Lou and Cowboy McCoy / by Barbara Larmon Failing ; pictures by Tedd Arnold.
p.   cm.
Summary: McCoy buys himself a cowboy hat, which leads to a new career and
a series of misadventures at the Bo-Dee-Oh Ranch.
ISBN 0-8037-2578-7
[1. Cowboys—Fiction. 2. Ranch life—Fiction. 3. Hats—Fiction. 4. Humorous stories.]
I. Arnold, Tedd, ill. II. Title.
PZ7.F1434 Las 2003   [E]—dc21   00-065888

The artwork was prepared using color pencils and watercolor washes.

This book is dedicated to Gates R. L. Failing,
who showed me which parts were funny.

—B.L.F.

For Jessica and Eileen—Happy trails!

—T.A.

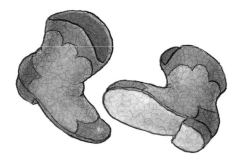

McCoy needed a new hat. He went to a store to get one.

"Do you have a hat for me?" McCoy asked the hat man.

"We have all kinds of hats," said the hat man. "A person's hat shows what he does. What kind of hat do you want?"

"I just want a hat that fits," said McCoy.

"Here's a firefighter hat," said the hat man. "Does that fit?"

McCoy tried it on. "Too big!" he said. "I guess I'm not going to put out fires."

"Here's a sailor hat," said the hat man. "Does that fit?"

"Too small!" said McCoy. "I guess I'm not going to sail the seas."

"Here's a chef hat," said the hat man. "Does that fit?"

"Too droopy!" said McCoy. "I guess I'm not going to cook for a crowd."

McCoy tried on a safari helmet, a coonskin cap, a straw hat, and a sombrero.

"Too hard! Too furry! Too itchy! Too wide!" proclaimed McCoy.

He tried on almost every cap and hat in the store. Nothing fit.

McCoy spotted one more hat on a high shelf. "Hey! How about that one?" he asked.

"That's a cowboy hat," said the hat man. "Are you a cowboy?"

"I don't know," said McCoy. "Let's see."

The hat man placed the
hat firmly on McCoy's head.

It was not too big.

It was not too small.

It was not too droopy.

It was not too hard, furry,
itchy, or wide.

"It fits!" cried McCoy.
"I *must* be a cowboy!"

McCoy paid for the hat and a spiffy new pair of boots. Then he ran out of the store. "I am Cowboy McCoy!" he shouted. "Which way to the ranch?"

Another cowboy came rushing down the street.

"I am Lasso Lou," he said. "I am running to catch the stagecoach for the Bo-Dee-Oh Ranch. Why don't you come with me?"

"Yahoo-ka-choo!" said Cowboy McCoy. "We can be cowboys together!"

Bumpity-bumpity—*thump-thump!* The stagecoach dropped

Lasso Lou and Cowboy McCoy at the Bo-Dee-Oh Ranch.

Lasso Lou brushed off his jeans. "I am glad to be off that

stagecoach."

"And I am glad not to be smooshed," cried Cowboy McCoy.

"Yahoo-ski-doo!"

Lasso Lou and Cowboy McCoy watched the foreman,

Smelly Mel, lead horses into the corral.

A horse nuzzled Lasso Lou. "I choose this horse," he said.

"Which one do you want, McCoy?"

"I don't want one," said Cowboy McCoy.

"McCoy," said Lasso Lou, "a cowboy must have a horse."

"I want seven horses," explained Cowboy McCoy.

"A cowboy only has one horse," said Lasso Lou.

"I *would* have one horse," said Cowboy McCoy. "One for each day of the week."

"NO!" cried Lasso Lou. "You must have the same horse for each day."

"Well, then," said Cowboy McCoy, "I'll just use your lasso and choose my one horse right now."

Cowboy McCoy tossed the lasso into the air. It landed on Smelly Mel.

"You can't ride Smelly Mel!" cried Lasso Lou.

"You're right," said Cowboy McCoy. He swung the lasso again. This time it landed on a chicken.

"You can't ride a chicken!" cried Lasso Lou.

"Hmm . . . probably not," said
Cowboy McCoy. He tried again.
The lasso landed on a pig.
"You can't ride a pig!" cried
Lasso Lou.

"Well . . . maybe I can," said
Cowboy McCoy.
The pig squealed and took
off across the corral—and
so did Cowboy McCoy.

The pig squealed and ran through a mud
puddle—and so did Cowboy McCoy.

He let go and he clamped his hat firmly on
his head. "I do not *want* to ride a pig," he said.

"Nice try, pardner," said Lou as he picked
up the lasso. He swung it over his head.
Whoosh! Whump! It landed on a horse.
"Do you like this horse?" he asked.

Cowboy McCoy smiled. "She's nice."

"I will call my horse Hero," said Lasso Lou.

"And I will call my horse SundayMondayTuesday-
WednesdayThursdayFridaySaturday," said Cowboy McCoy.

"That takes too long to say," said Lasso Lou.

"Then I will call her SundayMondayTuesdayWednesday-Thursday," declared Cowboy McCoy.

"NO! NO! NO!" cried Lasso Lou.

"Then I will call her YesterdayTodayTomorrow," said Cowboy McCoy.

"That's still too long," said Lasso Lou. "I know—what day is your favorite day?"

"Payday!" said Cowboy McCoy. "The day we get paid for being cowboys!"

"Payday! That's a fine name, McCoy," said Lasso Lou.

"Yahoo-a-roo!" cried Cowboy McCoy. "I have my horse!

Now I am a *real* cowboy."

"Do you know how to ride a horse?" asked Lasso Lou.

"Of course I do," said Cowboy McCoy.

Cowboy McCoy put his hands in the stirrups. "Lou?" he said. "I can't get on this saddle."

"You have to put your feet in the stirrups," said Lasso Lou.

"If I put my feet in the stirrups, I'll step on my hands,"
Cowboy McCoy explained.

"Your hands do not go in the stirrups!" Lasso Lou cried.

"Your feet go in the stirrups! And you need to sit on *top* of
Payday."

"Lou?" said Cowboy McCoy. "Payday's head is missing."

"Payday's head is at the front of the horse," said Lasso Lou.

"No, it is not," declared Cowboy McCoy. "And a cowboy cannot ride a horse with a missing head."

"I think you are facing the wrong way, McCoy," said Lasso Lou.

"Do you think so, Lou?" asked Cowboy McCoy.

"I do," said Lasso Lou.

Cowboy McCoy got off Payday. He found the front of his horse. Then he climbed back on top.

"Ready?" called Lasso Lou.

"Ready," said Cowboy McCoy.

"Now, how do we make them go and stop?"

"We say *giddyap* for go, and *whoa* for stop," Lasso Lou said.

"Yahoo-ma-goo!" shouted Cowboy McCoy. "GIDDYAP!"

Gal-lomp! Gal-lomp! Gal-lomp! Payday and Hero galloped across the prairie.

"Lou!" cried Cowboy McCoy. "How do you say this is the scariest ride of my life and I want it to stop RIGHT NOW!"

"Say *whoa!*" said Lasso Lou.

"WHOA!" cried Cowboy McCoy.

Hero and Payday stopped.

"I thought *whoa* meant stop," said Cowboy McCoy.

"It also means this is the scariest ride of my life and I want

it to stop—right now," explained Lasso Lou.

"Lou?" said Cowboy McCoy.

"Yes, McCoy?"

"How do you say I want to go back to the Bo-Dee-Oh Ranch and eat toasted marshmallows and cowboy punch?"

"Great idea, pardner!" said Lasso Lou. "Just say *giddyap*."

"GIDDYAP!" yelled Cowboy McCoy. "Yahoo-la-poo! Now we're ready to ride!"

Gal-lomp! Gal-lomp! Gal-lomp!

It was bedtime at the Bo-Dee-Oh Ranch.

Kaah-whew! Kaa-whew! Snort-snort!

Many tired cowboys snored in their bunks.

Lasso Lou was in a bottom bunk. Cowboy McCoy was on top.

"Good night, McCoy," said Lasso Lou.

"Good night, Lou," said Cowboy McCoy.

Suddenly Cowboy McCoy jumped down from his bunk.

"There is something scary up there!"

"What is it?" asked Lasso Lou.

"I do not know," said Cowboy McCoy. "But it is bumpy as a hill."

"Is it a hill?" asked Lasso Lou.

"No," said Cowboy McCoy.

"Because it is also humpy as a camel."

"Is it a camel?" asked Lasso Lou.

"No," said Cowboy McCoy.

"Because it is also lumpy as oatmeal."

"Is it oatmeal?" asked Lasso Lou

"No," said Cowboy McCoy.

"Because it is much scarier than oatmeal."

"You have a bumpy, humpy, lumpy thing in your bunk,"
said Lasso Lou.

"Yes!" cried Cowboy McCoy. "And please get it before it
bites me!" He dove under the covers with Lasso Lou.

Lasso Lou thought and thought.

Suddenly Cowboy McCoy screamed. "There it is!
It followed me!"

Lasso Lou stared at the scary thing. "McCoy, did you
take off your boots?"

"A cowboy *never* takes off his boots," declared
Cowboy McCoy.

"A cowboy *always* takes off his boots when it's time for
bed," explained Lasso Lou.

Cowboy McCoy climbed back up into his bunk. *Thud!*

Thud! His boots crashed to the floor.

"Lou?" said Cowboy McCoy.

"Yes?" said Lasso Lou.

"The bumpy, humpy, lumpy thing is gone."

"That's good, pardner," said Lasso Lou.